SEP — 2012

Kevin
Keeps Up

by Ann Whitehead Nagda

Holiday House/New York

HOLIDAY HOUSE is registered in the U.S. Patent and Trademark Office.
Printed and Bound in July 2012 at Maple Vail, York, PA USA.
First Edition
1 3 5 7 9 10 8 6 4 2
www.holidayhouse.com

Library of Congress Cataloging-in-Publication Data

Nagda, Ann Whitehead, 1945-
Kevin keeps up / by Ann Whitehead Nagda. — 1st ed.
p. cm.
Summary: When his teacher is replaced by a substitute nicknamed Beezer the
Buzzard, and each student has to do a report on an African animal, Kevin,
who struggles with attentional difficulties, is not sure he will survive the year.
ISBN 978-0-8234-2657-7 (hardcover)
[1. Attention—Fiction.   2. Teachers—Fiction.   3. Schools—Fiction.
4. Animals—Africa—Fiction.]   I. Title.
PZ7.N13355Ke 2012
[Fic]—dc23
2012002967

To Marilyn Malin,
with thanks
and love

chapter one

"My snake disappeared," Kevin announced as he hung up his coat at the back of the classroom.

"Bad news!" said Richard, unzipping his parka.

Jenny looked around nervously. "Is your snake somewhere in our classroom?"

"No," Kevin replied as he walked toward his desk. "Striker lives in my bedroom, but his cage was empty this morning." He fell heavily into his seat, which made his chair hit the desk behind him.

"Was that the snake you brought for the Valentine's Day party?" Jenny asked.

"No, that was Ratty." Kevin drummed his fingers on the desk.

Richard slid into his seat behind Jenny's. "Maybe Striker will show up when he gets hungry."

"When Ratty escaped, I never found him." Kevin sighed. He still missed Ratty.

Jenny shivered. "Are there a lot of loose snakes around your house?"

"No, but if my mother finds Striker before I do, her screams will be heard all over town." Kevin grimaced. His mother had never been very happy about his pet snakes.

"Scenes from a horror movie." Richard chuckled.

"It's not funny," said Kevin. "If Striker slithers out and scares my mother, I'll never be allowed to keep another snake in the house. Ever."

"Maybe you need a different kind of pet," said Jenny. "Something furry and cuddly."

"I like my pets slithery and scaly," said Kevin.

Jenny shivered again.

"Class, let's get started," said their teacher, Mrs. Steele. "We're going to begin a research project today."

Kevin groaned. He hated research projects. As if losing his snake wasn't enough bad news for one day.

Kevin swiveled in his chair so that he could watch Ruby, the tarantula. She was the class pet and had never escaped. Not yet anyway. This morning Ruby had climbed up the side of her cage using her sticky feet. Tarantulas have these great fangs they use to inject venom into their prey. Their fangs move up and down, kind of like Susan's hand when she wanted the teacher's attention, which was most of the time. She was doing it now. Richard had his hand up, too, but his arm was moving back and forth like a big wave to somebody far away.

Kevin leaned toward Jenny. "What was the question?"

Jenny frowned, then turned away.

Well, that wasn't very nice. Sometimes Kevin got the feeling that Jenny didn't like him. He was just trying to keep up with the classroom discussion.

Whatever the question was, Richard and Susan sure wanted to answer it. Which one would get called on? And the winner was Susan, otherwise known as Miss Smarty-pants.

"They are covered with hair," said Susan.

"That's right," said Mrs. Steele.

"Tarantulas have hairy legs and abdomens," Kevin said out loud.

Susan turned and gave him a dirty look. What a creep. He'd like to shoot a few tarantula hairs into her eyeball.

"Yes, tarantulas do have some hairs, but they're not mammals, are they?" His teacher stared at him with a pained look. Probably because he hadn't raised his hand. He forgot, okay? But then she said, "There is something else that all mammals do."

Richard's hand was waving again. Mammals could move their arms and hands all over the place.

Mrs. Steele nodded to Richard. She had to call on him before his arm fell off.

"Mammals feed milk to their babies," he said.

Kevin liked Richard. He was smart, but he wasn't a show-off like Susan.

"Good," said Mrs. Steele. "What are the glands called that produce milk for mammal babies?"

"Milk glands," Kevin said.

Mrs. Steele stared at him. She didn't say a thing.

Uh-oh. Was that the wrong answer? Or was his teacher unhappy that he hadn't raised his hand? Sometimes the words just came out of his mouth before he had a chance to even think about raising his hand.

"Kevin," his teacher said gently. "What's our class rule that you broke again?"

"Raise your hand," he muttered.

"Yes. Raise your hand before talking. And your answer is correct. Mammals have milk glands." Mrs. Steele wrote milk glands on the board.

Well, at least he had the right answer.

"What's another name for these glands?" Mrs. Steele asked.

He didn't know the answer to that one. This time only Susan raised her hand. "Mammary glands."

"Yes, only mammals have mammary glands. That's how these animals got the name *mammal*. Most mammals bear live young, but a few don't. They lay eggs instead. Can you name an egg-laying mammal?"

Susan had her hand up again, and Mrs. Steele nodded to her.

"A platypus." Susan had a smug look on her face.

Susan was a walking, talking encyclopedia. Kevin rolled his eyes at Jenny, and she smiled back. Maybe Jenny did like him. A little bit anyway.

"Right. That's an Australian mammal, isn't it?" Mrs. Steele began talking about where different mammals lived.

Kevin wished he could go somewhere like Australia and have an adventure. Someplace really exciting. Right now. If only he had his very own rocket ship and could blast off to the moon and beyond. He picked up his pencil and drew a rocket. It was zooming into the solar system. Oh no, there was an enemy ship. He fired at it with his laser gun. Now there were more enemy ships coming at him.

"Kevin," said his teacher, "what African mammal would you like to write about?"

Uh-oh. Did she say African animal? He zoomed his attention back from outer space and stared at the board. Someone had picked a gorilla. Probably Susan. The teacher's pet gorilla. Gorilla girl.

"What's your favorite mammal?" asked Mrs. Steele.

Kevin couldn't think of any favorite mammals. "I really like reptiles. Uh. And big hairy spiders like Ruby. But mammals..."

Susan turned and stared at him, frowning and wrinkling her nose. It made her two nostrils look really big, sort of like gorilla nostrils. Guess she didn't like snakes and spiders.

"Well, think about it some more and let me know later," said his teacher.

Richard raised his hand. "I'd like to write about wild dogs," he said.

That made sense. Richard talked about his old dog, Wolf, a lot. He was dog crazy.

Jenny wanted to write about leopards. No wonder. She loved cats. Her cat, Munchkin, was the official school cat. Munchkin often roamed the hallways, visiting a classroom or two. Then he'd take a nap on his special bench in the library.

Why did they have to write about mammals anyway? Kevin would much rather write about snakes.

Suddenly he heard his teacher say something about Africa.

"What was that?" he whispered to Jenny.

She shrugged, but Richard said softly, "She's going to Africa."

"This summer?" Kevin whispered.

"Next week!" Richard replied.

Kevin stared at his teacher. "Are we having a sub?" Oh no! He'd said it in his outside voice. And he'd forgotten to raise his hand. Now his teacher would give him a stern look.

But Mrs. Steele looked at him with kind eyes and said gently, "Mrs. Beezer will be your substitute teacher while I'm gone. She's excited to help all of you with your animal books."

Not the Beezer! Beezer the Buzzard! He was dead meat! Kevin put his head down on his desk with a clunk. The Buzzard would move his desk to the front of the room. She'd keep him in during recess. He wouldn't be able to share a joke with Richard or annoy Susan or anything. How could Mrs. Steele do this to him? How would he survive?

chapter two

After lunch recess it was time for silent reading. Kevin had a book open on his desk. The book had seemed okay in the beginning, but now he was bored with it. He pulled a blank piece of paper from his desk and began to draw the head of an anaconda with its

forked tongue sticking out. The snake smelled a substitute teacher. The teacher had black curly hair like Mrs. Beezer. Kevin grinned as he drew the big snake throwing its coils around her.

Suddenly, all around him, kids opened their desks, took out notebooks and pencils, and lined up by the door. Yikes! He was going to be left behind. Kevin rummaged around in his desk until he found his notebook, then grabbed a pencil and hurried after his classmates. He didn't know where they were headed. Sometimes he felt like a detective trying to solve a mystery. Right now the clues were the notebook, pencil, and no coats. Couldn't be outside for a field trip. Darn. Couldn't be art class either. The art teacher always gave them paper for their projects. Sometimes clay. He liked making monsters out of clay.

Mrs. Steele opened the door to the library. Oh no, not research.

As they entered the library the orderly line of students collapsed into a big bunch. Kevin was barely inside the door.

"Welcome, amigos." Nando, the librarian, walked toward them pushing a cart with books on it. "I've put some books about Africa on this cart. For nonfiction books about animals, you need to look in this section." He led them to some bookshelves. "And some of you might want to start by getting on a computer and using the Internet."

Kevin didn't like using the Internet. There was

just too much confusing stuff. He liked short books with lots of pictures.

"Let me know if you need help," Nando said. He looked right at Kevin when he said it.

Kevin had noticed Nando's shiny brown cowboy boots, so he said, "Cool boots."

"Thanks, amigo." The librarian winked and then turned to help Richard with something.

Kevin knew he needed help, but not with mammals. He needed help persuading Mrs. Steele to let him write about snakes. But Nando probably wouldn't be much help with that.

All around him kids were grabbing books from the shelves. Kevin sat on the floor and started reading titles. Camels, Foxes, Giraffes, Gorillas. He looked around for Gorilla Girl, but she had disappeared. Probably on a computer. He pulled a book about gorillas from the shelf and paged through it, looking at the pictures. They sure had huge, funny-looking noses. The big guys looked downright grumpy. Gorilla Girl would fit right in.

"That looks like an interesting book." Mrs. Steele knelt beside him and pointed at one of the pictures. "My, that's a handsome-looking silverback. Would you like to write about gorillas, too?"

"No way." He didn't want anything to do with Gorilla Girl. Kevin snapped the book shut. "I thought Susan might like to read it."

Mrs. Steele smiled at him and took the book. "I'll show it to Susan. That was nice of you to think of her.

I'd like everyone in our class to help each other, so each student can create a great animal book."

Kevin opened his mouth and stared at his teacher. "We have to make real books?"

His teacher nodded. "Oh yes, with text and pictures and at least one graph."

"That sounds like a lot of work!" Kevin had a sick feeling in his stomach.

"Don't worry. You'll be spending several weeks on it."

Kevin moaned.

Mrs. Steele patted his shoulder. "I'll help you get started. Do you think you might be interested in learning about cheetahs? I know a lot about them because my husband is in Africa right now studying cheetahs."

Kevin looked up at her. "Is that why you're going to Africa?"

"Yes, I haven't seen my husband for six weeks," said his teacher.

"That's a long time," said Kevin. "I guess you miss him."

"Yes, I do." Mrs. Steele smiled at him and plucked two cheetah books from the shelf. "Read about cheetahs and see what you think. Take the books home with you tonight so you can decide whether you want to research cheetahs or some other mammal."

Kevin sighed. He was certainly going to miss his teacher. He stood up holding the books and tried to decide what to do next.

Richard sat by a computer. When he saw Kevin, he motioned to him. "Look what I found. I Googled 'escaped snakes,' and here's a whole article about it." Richard pointed to some words on the screen.

Kevin sat down beside him and studied the screen. "Wow! There are a lot of words. Did you read it?"

"Yeah. It says to sprinkle flour on the floor, and if the snake crawls through it, you'll be able to tell what room they're in."

"You mean sprinkle flour in every room?" Kevin asked.

Richard nodded. "Especially in doorways or near places a snake might hide."

"My mother will love that!" Kevin rolled his eyes. He sure had a lot to do once he got home. He had to read two books, finish the math work sheet he hadn't finished in class, and secretly sprinkle flour all over the house.

chapter three

The next morning Kevin was bleary-eyed when he got to school. As soon as he staggered to his desk and sat down, Richard asked, "Did you find your snake?"

Kevin shook his head. "Not yet, but I think Striker is in the living room. He crawled through the flour by the couch."

"Did you search behind and inside of everything in the room?" Richard asked.

"Well, sort of. But it was four in the morning, and I had to sweep up the flour."

Jenny looked at him like he was some kind of alien creature. "You were up at four in the morning sweeping flour?"

"Yes. I didn't want my mother to see it," Kevin told her. "She's pretty fussy about having clean floors."

Jenny raised her eyebrows. "How did the flour get on the floor?"

Kevin knew it sounded like he was crazy. "I sprinkled it around the house at midnight."

Richard laughed, which made Kevin start to laugh, too.

Jenny just looked puzzled.

Kevin didn't get a chance to explain, because the principal began to make the morning announcements. Kevin began to worry about the flour. What if his mother found some he'd missed and decided to clean the house? She might find the snake if she moved the furniture to vacuum. He should have spent more time searching the living room, but he'd been so tired. He put his head down on his desk.

Kevin sat up straight when he heard Mrs. Steele say, "I want each of you to write an introductory paragraph or two about your animal."

Oh no. Writing was hard enough when he was wide-awake.

His teacher continued, "Use as many of your senses as you can. What does your animal look like? What kind of sounds does it make? Lions roar and elephants trumpet."

"Arf, arf."

The sound came from behind Kevin. He looked around. Wild Dog Richard was grinning.

"Thank you, Richard," said Mrs. Steele. "Now, the other three senses are smell, taste, and feel. Does your animal have a particular smell? For example, cats mark their territories with scented urine."

"The lion yard in the zoo really stinks," said Jenny.

"Yes, it does," agreed Mrs. Steele. "Can you describe the smell?"

"It's really strong and makes you want to run the other way." Jenny wrinkled her nose.

Mrs. Steele laughed. "It's a strong, musky smell, isn't it? Remembering that smell probably made you remember other things about your day at the zoo. By describing how things smell or sound or taste or feel, and not just how they look, you can really make your writing come alive."

Kevin shuddered. This writing business kept getting more complicated. He flipped through one of the cheetah books. Lots of pictures. No sounds or smells. He looked at some more pictures. He saw two cheetahs on a tree. The text by the picture said, "Cheetah Cubs." He had to admit they were awfully cute. Even if they were cats.

Mrs. Steele leaned over him. "Are you having trouble getting started?"

He nodded.

"Why don't you write each of the five senses in your notebook?" said his teacher. "Leave room for note-taking beneath each one. Then read your two books about cheetahs again. Write down some words or phrases the author uses to describe each sense."

Kevin hadn't even read the books once. But he certainly wasn't going to tell that to his teacher. He wrote "See," "Hear," "Smell," and "Feel" on a page in his notebook. He wondered what a cheetah's fur felt like. He'd like to pat a cheetah at the zoo. But that was probably a good way to lose a hand. He only had four senses on his paper. What was the last one? He looked up at the board. Taste. He certainly didn't want to taste a cheetah! He wrote "Taste" down anyway, just to make Mrs. Steele happy.

Now he'd have to read at least one of the books. He opened the book that had big print and not too many

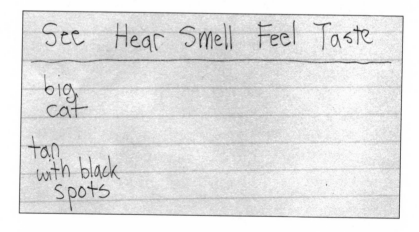

words. On the first page of the book, the author used the words "big cat" and "tan with black spots." Kevin wrote those words under See. He read that cheetahs also have two black stripes on their faces that go from their eyes to their mouth. He wrote that down, too. But the book didn't say anything about the other senses. The author had obviously never had Mrs. Steele for a teacher.

He picked up the other book. Guess he'd have to read it after all. Yuck! The book had small print and lots of words. He paged through the book. Luckily, it had headings at the top of the page, so he didn't have to read every page. Wow! They had a whole page on cheetah sounds. There was a big picture of a cheetah growling. Its teeth looked big and sharp. He read that cheetahs also purr. They purr so loudly that you can still hear them twenty feet away. He wrote "purr" and "growl" on his paper.

The next sense was smell. Is a cheetah smelly? He had no idea.

Kevin leaned toward Jenny. "Does your cat stink?"

"No." Jenny scowled at him.

Maybe she didn't like being interrupted. But she'd been staring into space. He looked at her notebook. She hadn't written anything either.

Mrs. Steele was by his side again. "How are you doing?"

Kevin sighed. "I can't find anything about how cheetahs feel or smell. Do we have to use all five senses?"

"Why don't you try to use three senses." His teacher leaned over his desk. "Let's look in your book for any words that describe how something feels or smells. Oh, here's a description of a cheetah's tongue."

Kevin read the words where his teacher's fingers were pointing. "The long tongue is covered with tiny rasps." He looked up at his teacher. "What's a rasp?"

"What do you think it might be?" Mrs. Steele asked.

"Something bumpy?"

"Let's look it up." Mrs. Steele walked to her desk and came back with a dictionary. Maybe she didn't know what the word meant either.

His teacher flipped the pages until she found the word. " 'A rasp is a coarse file with cutting points.' "

"What's a coarse file?"

"A carpenter might use a file on some wood. Let's look up the word 'coarse.' " His teacher could find things really fast in the dictionary. "See here. It has several meanings. Coarse can mean 'loose or rough in texture.' That's the meaning we want here."

Kevin quickly wrote "rough" and "tiny rasps" in his notebook. "Can I say the tongue of a cheetah is rough with tiny rasps all over it?"

"Sure," said Mrs. Steele, "but use something else instead of rasps in case other students don't know what that is."

"A cheetah's tongue is rough. It's covered with tiny pointy things."

"And what do those pointy things help a cheetah do?"

"They help the cheetah comb dirt out of its fur and lick bits of meat off bones."

"Great," said Mrs. Steele. "Write all that down and you'll have a good paragraph. I'll be eager to see your finished book when I come back from Africa." His teacher gave him a big smile before she walked away to help Eliseo with his writing.

Kevin gulped. He wasn't sure he'd be able to write anything when Mrs. Steele was gone.

Jenny leaned toward him. "My book says a leopard's tongue is rough, too," she said in a low voice, "but it doesn't say anything about rasps."

"You're lucky," said Kevin.

"You should be working on your introductory paragraphs now," said Mrs. Steele.

Uh-oh. Kevin turned to a fresh page in his notebook. He wrote "Cheetahs" at the top of the page. He wasn't sure what to write first. He looked over at Jenny's notebook. She had written, "Leopards are big cats. They have spots on their fur. The spots help them blend in with trees and grass."

Kevin wrote, "Cheetahs are big tan cats. They have black spots all over their fur." He hadn't copied Jenny's writing exactly. He'd used different words. Well, sort of. It was just so hard to get started. Now he could write what he'd worked on with Mrs. Steele. "A cheetah's tongue is rough. It is covered with tiny pointy things. They help the cheetah comb its fur or lick meat off bones." Two senses down. One more to go. He tapped his foot while he tried to think of something else to write.

"Shhhh!" Jenny hissed at him. "You're making too much noise."

Kevin had noticed that Jenny got crabby when she had to write something. He felt crabby, too, but tapping helped him think. And noise was exactly what he needed to write about. He stopped tapping and moved his knee back and forth while he thought some more.

Munchkin hopped onto Jenny's desk. Jenny rubbed the cat's ears, and he started to purr.

That's right, Kevin thought, cheetahs purr just like pet house cats. Thank you, Munchkin. He wrote, "Cheetahs purr when they're happy and growl when they're mad."

Cheetahs are big tan cats. They have black spots all over their fur. A cheetah's tongue is rough. It is covered with tiny pointy things. They help the cheetah comb its fur or lick meat off bones. Cheetahs purr when they're happy and growl when they're mad.

Kevin thought about his snake again. Striker didn't make any noise when he was happy, but he hissed when he was mad. He hoped Striker wasn't hissing at his mother or she'd be growling when he got home.

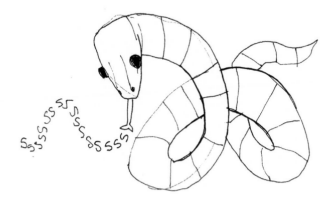

chapter four

As Kevin entered the school on Monday and walked down the hall, he thought about Mrs. Steele. She should be in Africa now, but maybe her plane broke on Saturday and she had to stay home. Or maybe Mrs. Beezer was sick. He entered the classroom and looked around. No teacher at all. So far so good.

He walked back to his cubby to hang up his jacket. "Have you seen the Buzzard yet?" he asked as Richard walked by.

Richard dropped his backpack into a cubby and gave Kevin a strange look. "The buzzard?"

"That's what I call Mrs. Beezer," Kevin explained.

Richard laughed, then put out both arms and flapped to his desk.

Moments later Mrs. Beezer strode into the room. She carried a canvas bag, which she dropped by Mrs. Steele's desk. The bag hit the floor with a thud. Kevin sank into his seat. He was sure the bag contained the bones of her recent victims.

"Okay, class, let's get started. We have a lot to do today." Beezer the Buzzard gave the class one of her little half smiles. Her face would crack if she really smiled. "I'm Mrs. Beezer. You all know me because I've substituted in your classroom before."

Kevin knew her all right. He felt his jaw clench.

"Mrs. Steele told me all about your African animal project. Last week you wrote about your animal's appearance," Mrs. Beezer continued. "Today you're going to come up with a page of math about your animal."

Math! Did she say math?

"Get out one of your animal books from the library. Can you find some interesting numbers in there?"

Kevin pulled out a book and flipped through it. Yeah, there were some page numbers.

Susan raised her hand. "A silverback gorilla can weigh five hundred pounds, while a female only weighs two hundred pounds."

"Good." Beezer the Buzzard looked at Susan, then studied a piece of paper. "Thank you, Susan. So, class, for example you can compare the weights of the male and female animals. You can also compare your animal's weight with that of other animals in the same family."

"Like how a gorilla compares with other great apes, like chimpanzees and orangutans," Susan said.

"Exactly. And what would be a good way to show the different weights on your math page?"

"You could use a graph," said Susan.

Oh, joy. Kevin hated graphs almost as much as he hated Susan when she was acting like a know-it-all.

"Can someone give me an example of other animals in your family?" The Buzzard looked around for a victim.

Susan's real family would have werewolves and vampires in it. Kevin started drawing a picture of a werewolf with rosebud earrings in its ears.

"We could compare leopards, lions, and cheetahs," said Jenny.

"That's a great idea." The Beezer looked down at her paper again. "Let's see. You're Jenny, aren't you? And you're writing about leopards." She gave Jenny one of her crooked smiles. "So you could get together with Rana, the 'lion' student, and Kevin, the 'cheetah' student, to do a graph, couldn't you?"

Oh, wonderful. Now he was a "cheetah" student. And he was in the same family as Lion Girl and Leopard Girl. But maybe they'd do all the work. That wouldn't be so bad.

Munchkin walked into the room and jumped up on Jenny's desk.

With lightning speed the Buzzard swooped down and grabbed the cat with her shiny red talons. Then she held him out like a smelly lump of garbage. "What is this cat doing at school?"

"He's our school cat," said Jenny. "His name is Munchkin."

"He doesn't belong in our classroom," the Buzzard said as she thrust the cat into the hall, then quickly closed the door.

Kevin decided he would lure Munchkin into the classroom as often as possible.

"I have graph paper on my desk." Mrs. Beezer waved a stack of papers in the air. "Now you can either get together with the other members of your animal family or you can make a graph on your own."

No way did Kevin want to work on his own. He

scooted his chair next to Jenny's. Rana moved to the other side of Jenny's desk.

Richard moaned. "I don't have a family. I'm the only dog."

Kevin leaned back and put one hand on Richard's desk. "You could be an honorary cat."

"Or maybe an ornery cat." Richard smirked.

Suddenly the Buzzard landed beside them. "Boys, are you working on your graphs or are you just chatting?"

Kevin turned around and sat up straight.

"You're Kevin, aren't you?" Mrs. Beezer had the seating chart in her hand again. "I'm going to keep my eye on you today."

That's what a real buzzard would do, Kevin thought. It would watch potential prey very carefully. Unfortunately, he was the prey.

"First we need to find the weights of our animals," said Rana. "An average female lion is about three hundred pounds and a male is four hundred and fifty."

Kevin picked up his book and leafed through it. "I can't find anything about cheetah weights."

Rana sighed and held out her hand. "Let me look in your book. You can go and get some graph paper."

Kevin made his way to the front of the room, stopping to talk with Eliseo along the way. He picked up several graph sheets from the teacher's desk and flapped them over Mary's head. When she glared at him, he did it again. He looked up and saw the Buzzard watching him, so he hurried back to his chair and sat down.

"Okay, a male cheetah weighs about one hundred and twenty-five pounds and a female weighs one hundred pounds," Rana told him.

"That's almost the same as a leopard," said Jenny. "Did you know that a leopard can climb a tree with a dead animal in its mouth? And the dead animal can weigh more than the leopard does."

"That sounds impossible," said Kevin. "There's no way I could pull Richard up a tree, and he weighs about as much as I do."

"Hey, wait a minute," said Richard. "I wouldn't let you pull me up a tree."

"I read that cheetahs can hardly climb trees at all," said Rana.

"My book doesn't say that," said Kevin.

"Yes it does." Rana grabbed his cheetah book, flipped through it, and pointed at the bottom of a page. "Here it is. 'Cheetah cubs can climb trees easily, but adult cheetahs can't.' So there."

That made him feel really stupid. Kevin took his book and moved back to his own desk. Then he started reading the book again from the beginning, trying to find something that cheetahs did better than leopards or lions.

Suddenly the Buzzard was beside him again. "Where's your graph, Kevin?"

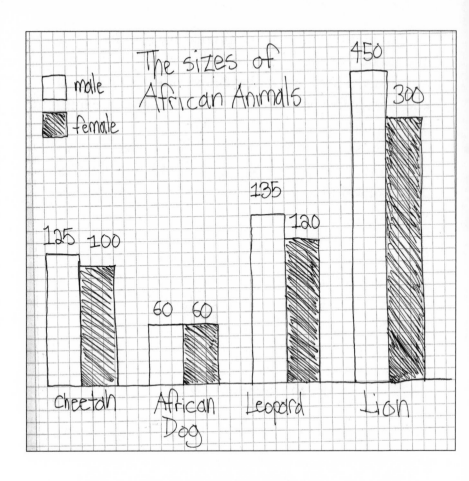

The sizes of African Animals

male
female

125 100

60 60

135 120

450 300

Cheetah
African Dog
Leopard
Lion

"Right there," Kevin pointed to Jenny's desk.

"No." The Buzzard shook her head. "You didn't have a thing to do with that graph. You will do your *own* graph during recess this morning."

Kevin put his head down on the desk.

When the rest of the class left for recess, Kevin worked on his graph. Jenny had given him her completed graph, so all he had to do was copy it. He had almost finished when the Buzzard was called to the office. He hoped the principal would fire her for incredible meanness. He walked to the front of the room to sharpen his pencil, then walked by her desk. On top of Mrs. Steele's planning book was a letter to Mrs. Beezer. At the bottom of the page, she had written, "Please feel free to contact me via e-mail if you have any questions or problems." And she had written her e-mail address. Kevin grabbed a piece of graph paper and copied it. He had lots of problems. And questions, too.

Somehow he made it to the end of the day without getting into more trouble. As soon as he got home from school, he got on the Internet and wrote an e-mail to his teacher.

> Dear Mrs. Steele,
>   Why did you go away? Mrs. Beezer is mean to me. Do leopards really climb trees better than cheetahs?
>   Your sad student,
>   Kevin

chapter five

On Tuesday morning Kevin logged on to the computer before going to school. There was an e-mail from Mrs. Steele. She had written:

> Dear Kevin,
>   I'm sorry you're having trouble in class. My husband says that cheetahs have trouble climbing trees because their claws are not sharp. Most other cats, including leopards, have protective pockets they can pull their claws into, but cheetahs don't. A cheetah's paws aren't much good for doing anything except running.
>   Your concerned teacher,
>   Mrs. Steele

It was comforting to hear from his teacher. Kevin read the e-mail again. He printed the message out, folded it up, and put it in his pocket. Then he glanced at the clock. Oh no, he was going to be late for school. He grabbed his backpack and a banana and rushed out the door.

By the time he reached his classroom, the Buzzard was calling roll. Fortunately, she hadn't called his name yet. When she did, he mumbled, "Here." She stared at him for a long moment. It was the kind of stare an African vulture might make before swooping down and grabbing a small, helpless creature in its sharp talons.

He raised his hand to buy the school lunch, even though it was fish fingers. He didn't like them, but it was better than nothing. He wondered why the sticks of fish were called fingers. After all, fish didn't have any fingers. They had fins, but fish fins probably didn't taste much better than fingers.

The Beezer said, "This morning you're going to write about your animal's diet."

Kevin frowned. Whenever his mother went on a diet, they didn't have anything good to eat for a while. He didn't think animals went on that kind of diet.

Now the Beezer was writing something on the board. Her printing wasn't very good and all the words sloped downhill. Kevin squinted and read, "What does your animal eat? How does it find food?" Well, that didn't seem too hard. He searched inside his desk for a piece of paper and a pencil. Then he wrote, "A cheetah kills animals and eats them." He couldn't think of anything else to write. He rolled his pencil back and forth on his desk.

Kevin looked around. Susan was writing and writing. He'd seen a movie about gorillas, and they were eating leaves. How many sentences did it take to say that?

Beside him Jenny was looking through a book. She was looking at a picture of a leopard. He leaned over to get a better look. The leopard was in a tree eating an animal. The animal's legs were hanging on either side of the tree limb.

"Kevin, have you finished your work already?" Suddenly the Buzzard was next to him. "Move your arm so I can see your paper." She leaned over him. "You need to write more than that," she said.

Kevin looked up at her and said, "I can't think of anything else to write."

"Get out your book about cheetahs and read it again."

Kevin looked in his desk and then his backpack. He'd left both of his cheetah books at home. He swung one leg back and forth. Jenny wrote something on her paper. Kevin leaned over to read it. It said, "Leopards eat wildebeests, gazelles, baby giraffes, porcupines, and even dung beetles."

"What's a dung beetle?" Kevin asked.

"It's a beetle that eats poop," said Richard.

"Yuck!" Kevin turned around and stared at Richard.

Suddenly the Buzzard was beside him. "Kevin, move your desk to the front of the room."

"N-N-No, you don't understand," Kevin stammered. "I was just trying to find out what leopards eat because maybe cheetahs eat the same thing, since they're the same size as leopards."

"Why aren't you looking for information in a book?"

"I left my cheetah books at home by mistake."

"Move your desk." This time the Buzzard pointed a long talon toward the front of the room.

Kevin stood and began pushing his desk. It hit Mary's desk, and his pencil rolled onto the floor. He stooped to pick up the pencil.

The Buzzard grabbed the front of his desk and moved it beside her big desk. "Get your chair," she ordered. "And then sit down and write."

Kevin knew he was dead meat. He'd never be able to finish his animal book when he was sitting so close to the mean, kid-eating vulture. He stared at the blackboard. He could hear noises behind him, but he couldn't see any of his classmates. He twirled his pencil on the desk. The Buzzard glared at him. He stopped twirling and picked up his pencil. But his mind was blank. He was glad when the Buzzard left her perch and flew away. He turned his head and saw her standing over Eliseo. Uh-oh. Another victim.

Instead, she smiled. Well, at least she showed her teeth. "Eliseo, I like what you've written. And this math fact is great. Read this sentence to the class." Using a sharp red fingernail, she tapped a spot on his paper.

Eliseo read slowly. "A hyena can eat up to forty pounds of meat at one time."

"You can use that fact for your diet math page. You can compare how much a hyena eats with how much another predator eats. Has anyone else found out how much their animal can eat?" The Buzzard looked all around the room. No one raised a hand. Not even Susan.

Mrs. Beezer looked at the clock. "Class, it's time for recess. Everyone line up, please."

Kevin stood up.

"Not you, Kevin. No recess for you until you write some more."

Kevin slumped into his chair and shut his eyes. That meant no recess until Mrs. Steele came back. He felt someone tap his shoulder. He looked up, and Richard dropped a folded piece of paper on his desk. Kevin quickly moved the paper to his lap. Unfolding it, he read, "I think cheetahs like to eat gazelles." Kevin didn't really know what gazelles were, but he was grateful to Richard for trying to help. He needed all the help he could get.

chapter six

At lunch Kevin wrapped two of his fish fingers in a napkin. He planned to break the fish into little pieces and lay a trail of fish from the hall into his classroom. Maybe he could get Munchkin to pay a surprise visit to the class.

But after lunch there were too many people in the hall. If he laid a fish trail, all the kids would walk through the fish and get it on their shoes. The fishy trail would lead everywhere.

Kevin didn't have to return to his desk in the front of the room, because the Beezer lined them up right away to go to the library. They were supposed to do research on the Internet.

As he entered the library Nando pulled him aside. "I found an interesting film about African predators," he told Kevin. "Would you like to watch it?"

"Sure." Kevin was surprised. This was much

better than getting on a computer and having the Buzzard breathing down his neck.

A big TV sat on a cart in the librian's office. Nando motioned to the chair by his desk. "Have a seat." He put in a DVD and started the film.

Kevin sat down, then set the napkin holding the fish fingers on the desk.

"Oh, here comes Munchkin," said Nando.

The cat jumped up on the desk and sniffed the napkin, then grabbed it with his claws and shook it. The fish fingers tumbled onto the table, and the cat began to gulp them down.

"I hope that wasn't your afternoon snack," said Nando.

"No, I brought the fish for Munchkin." Kevin touched the soft fur on the cat's head with his finger. The cat rubbed the side of his face on Kevin's hand.

Nando handed him some paper. "When the movie ends, you might want to draw a few important scenes before you write anything."

"I usually get yelled at when I draw stuff," said Kevin.

"Don't worry. I won't yell at you," said Nando as he started the movie. "Some students find that drawing something first can help them figure out what to write."

While Kevin watched the movie Munchkin climbed into his lap and went to sleep. Kevin tried to keep his legs still so he wouldn't wake the cat up. He thrumbed his fingers on the desk as he watched the cheetah chase a skinny brown animal with long legs and a dark stripe on its side.

After the movie ended, Kevin drew a picture of a cheetah standing on a hill. Then, he drew a cheetah chasing an animal, and finally, he drew the cheetah eating. Then he wrote fast so he could get everything he remembered down on paper. His hand hurt when he finished.

Nando came back in the office and patted the sleeping cat. "I see you've made a friend."

Kevin smiled. He'd enjoyed watching the movie with a warm kitty on his lap. "I think Munchkin likes me," said Kevin.

"Keep bringing him treats and he'll love you forever," said the librarian.

The cat jumped off Kevin's lap, rubbed against Nando's leg, then left the office. "Did you like the movie?"

"It was good," said Kevin.

Nando sat down next to Kevin. "I really like your drawings. Now tell me what you've learned about cheetahs and how they catch their food."

Kevin read from his paper. "The cheetah stood on a hill for a long time and watched animals. It saw something it liked, so it crawled through the grass, then suddenly ran very fast. The animal, a gazelle, tried to get away, but it couldn't. The cheetah knocked it down and then held its throat."

"That's to keep it from breathing, right?" said Nando. "So the gazelle suffocates."

"Yeah. That's a lot more than I wrote this morning."

"I like what you've written," said Nando. "Did you learn anything else about cheetahs?"

"Lions sometimes steal from cheetahs," said Kevin.

Nando thought a minute. "Maybe you could write, 'Lions sometimes steal a cheetah's kill.'"

Kevin nodded happily and wrote the new sentence down. "You know, while she was eating, the cheetah mom looked around a lot."

"Did the cheetah have any cubs with her?" Nando asked.

Kevin nodded. "One small cub was next to the mom. They both had bloody faces. Cheetahs sure are messy eaters."

Nando laughed. "Your face would be messy, too, if you ate by sticking your mouth in your food."

He stood up. "Mrs. Beezer left with your classmates a few minutes ago, so you'd better go, too."

Kevin wrote two more sentences before hurrying back to his classroom.

He handed what he'd written to the Buzzard. "Can I move my desk back where it belongs now?" he asked.

"Let me read it first." She frowned as she read it. "I can barely make out some of the words." She pointed to the paper. "I can't read this sentence at all. What does it say?"

> The cheetah stood on a hill for a long time and watched animals. It saw something it liked, so it crawled through the grass, then suddenly ran very fast. The animal, a gozelle, tried to get away, but it couldn't. The cheetah knocked it down and then held its throat.
> Lions sometimes steal a cheetah's kill.

Kevin looked where she was pointing. It was what he had written about the cheetahs' bloody faces. He read it to the Buzzard.

"Don't you think that's awfully gory?"

"But that's the way it was in the movie."

The Buzzard shook her head. "Maybe you could leave that part out. You can move your desk back after you write this again neatly."

Beezer the Buzzard was impossible, Kevin thought. She'd never be satisfied with anything he did. He missed Mrs. Steele more every day.

As soon as Kevin got home, he wrote an e-mail to his teacher.

Dear Mrs. Steele,
    Today Mrs. Beezer made me stay in from recess again because I didn't write enough about a cheetah's diet. Then Nando showed me a movie, so I wrote a lot more, but Mrs. Beezer still didn't like it.
    Your depressed student,
    Kevin

PS How much can a cheetah eat?

Chapter Seven

The next morning Kevin checked his e-mail as soon as he got up. Mrs. Steele had written back.

> Dear Kevin,
>   Your question is a good one, but I don't know the answer. Right now I have to hurry off to feed some of the animals at the center. Try a Google search on the computer and see if you can find the answer yourself. Let me know what you find out.
>   Your concerned teacher,
>   Mrs. Steele

Oh no. Mrs. Steele didn't answer his question. She was still expecting him to do a good job without her. He didn't think he could do it. He wondered if the

Buzzard would make him move his desk next to hers again. Maybe if he lured Munchkin into the classroom, she'd forget all about his missing math page.

After Kevin ate a bowl of cereal, he went into the pantry and looked around. All he could find was a can of tuna fish. He didn't particularly like it, but maybe the cat would. He set the can on the kitchen counter and wrestled two slices of bread out of their plastic wrapper.

His mother gave him a puzzled look. "I thought you hated tuna fish."

"No, I like it. I'm making a sandwich for my lunch." Kevin reached for the can opener. As the blade punctured the metal lid Kevin smelled the fishy odor. This would be even better than fish fingers for luring the cat into his classroom. He grabbed a small plastic bag, scooped some of the tuna inside, and stuffed the bag into his pocket. After dumping the rest of the fish into a bowl, he mixed in mayonnaise, then spread the tuna on a piece of bread and put another slice of bread on top. Yummy. If you liked tuna. Maybe he could trade sandwiches with someone. He put the sandwich in a plastic bag and put it in his backpack.

When Kevin got to school, he hurried into the library, looking for the cat. Munchkin was stretched out on the cushion of his favorite chair. Kevin took the tuna bag out of his pocket and noticed that some tuna juice had leaked on his pants. He'd smell like a big fish all day long. Well, maybe the smell would keep the Buzzard away. He put a small glob of tuna on his finger and held it next to the cat's nose. Munchkin sniffed the tuna, then ate it, cleaning every last bit off Kevin's finger with his pink tongue. It felt like sandpaper. Kevin wondered if a cheetah's tongue was a lot rougher than that. "There's more for you, my furry friend," he said, swinging the bag with the remaining tuna in front of the cat. As Kevin turned and walked toward the hallway, the cat jumped down and followed him.

The Buzzard was talking to Susan, so she didn't notice the cat walking into the classroom. Munchkin followed Kevin to his cubby. The cat sniffed his backpack. "I bet you smell my sandwich, don't you?" He leaned over to pat the cat's head, but the cat batted at the tuna bag. Kevin pulled the bag away. "Follow the yummy smell," he said.

Sure enough, the cat followed him to his seat and jumped into his lap. Munchkin sniffed the tuna stain on Kevin's pants, then reached a paw toward the plastic bag. Kevin dumped the rest of the tuna into his hand and fed it to the cat. After gulping down the tuna, the cat licked the palm of Kevin's hand over and over with his sandpaper tongue. It tickled.

"My cat really likes you." Jenny sounded surprised.

"Your cat really likes my tuna fish," Kevin told her.

Munchkin purred.

Jenny sat down, then leaned toward Kevin and whispered, "Maybe Mrs. Beezer hasn't noticed the cat yet."

"She watches me like a hawk," said Kevin. "She'll probably spot the cat pretty soon."

Richard slid into his seat. "What's the big secret?"

Kevin turned around and pointed to his lap.

Richard raised his eyebrows. "It's the cat who shouldn't be in our classroom."

"Okay, class, everyone take your seats." Mrs. Beezer stood up and started handing out graph paper. "It's time to get started with a math activity. I noticed that many of you were having trouble making graphs for your animal books. So this morning we're going to find out which animal is the most popular pet in this class. Then I want each of you to make a bar graph."

What? More graphs! Kevin groaned.

"First we're going to gather some information," said the sub. "Please raise your hand if you have a pet dog."

Lots of hands went up.

The Buzzard wrote the word "dogs" on the board and next to it she wrote "6." "Now raise your hand if you have a cat."

Even more hands were raised. Cats were certainly popular. Eight students had them.

When the sub asked about fish, only four students raised their hands. And two students had rodents. The Buzzard didn't ask about reptiles. Kevin shrugged. She probably didn't consider snakes a proper pet. Kevin wouldn't have known whether to raise his hand or not anyway. His snake was still missing.

Kevin found the weight graph he'd copied from

Jenny. The pet graph was easier because it didn't need such big numbers. He counted up eight squares and drew the bar for cats. When he'd finished drawing the four bars, he had lots of space at the top of the paper, so he drew a picture of a cat standing on his hind legs with his front paws in the air like he was cheering. Across the cat's chest he wrote "The Winner." Then

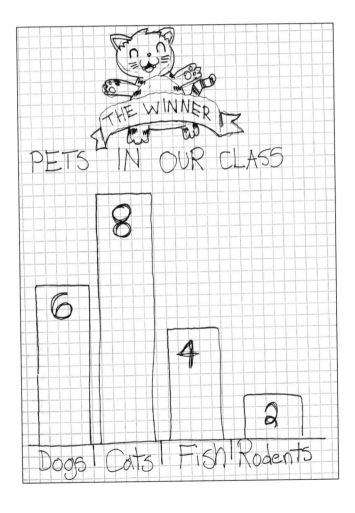

he ran his fingers along Munchkin's soft fur. He still liked snakes, but they didn't snuggle on your lap or purr when you fed them.

The Buzzard was suddenly standing beside him. "Take that cat back to the library right now," she growled.

Kevin held the sleepy cat close to his chest as he rushed out of the room. Obviously, the Buzzard didn't like cats. She didn't like him much either.

chapter eight

It was Friday morning. Almost the end of a terrible week. Kevin slumped in his seat and hoped for a sudden heavy snowstorm so school would be dismissed early. Out the window the sky was cloudy, but no snowflakes were falling. It was probably too warm.

Mrs. Beezer stood in front of the room with a huge smile on her face. She held a piece of paper in her hand. Kevin hoped she'd won the lottery and was taking a long vacation to someplace far away. Maybe she was leaving today and had written a letter to say good-bye. Then another sub would take her place. Anyone would be better than the Buzzard.

"I just received an e-mail from Mrs. Steele." The Buzzard glanced around the room to be sure everyone was paying attention. Her eyes stopped roving and rested on Kevin for a moment. He sat up straighter and stopped jiggling his pencil. "Dear class," the teacher read. "Today was our most exciting day so far. We watched a cheetah named Peaches run in a grassy field. She accelerated like a race car, her feet thudding on the dirt path."

Kevin thought Peaches was a dumb name for a speedy cheetah. She should be named Rocket or Lightning. The Buzzard continued to read. "During part of each stride Peaches seemed to fly through the air with all four legs off the ground. When she went by me, she was a blur of tan fur and black spots. She seemed to be running for the sheer joy of it."

Kevin wondered what it would be like to run like that. He ran fast during soccer or baseball, but that wasn't joyful running. That was running under pressure. He tuned back in for the end of the e-mail. "Of course, Becky, her trainer, gave Peaches some meat as a reward when she finished her run. It was a thrill to be so close to a running cheetah."

The Beezer looked up. "Isn't that fun?" she said. "Don't you wish you were there watching those racing cheetahs?"

Kevin wished with all his might that he could be in Africa with Mrs. Steele.

"I wish I had chosen cheetahs," grumbled Mike. "They're the best animal."

Cheetahs *were* really special. Kevin was lucky to be writing about them. Unfortunately, his writing wasn't very good. If he were in Africa with Mrs. Steele, maybe he could make his cheetah book special. With the Beezer he couldn't seem to do anything but get in trouble.

Susan raised her hand. "Yes, Susan," said the teacher.

"Cheetahs can run seventy miles an hour," she said.

How dare Susan give information about his animal! "Cheetahs are the fastest land animals," Kevin said loudly.

The Beezer gave him one of her deadly stares.

Kevin stared right back at her.

"That's right," she finally said. "They're very fast." Then she glanced at the clock. "Now it's time for your physical education class. Line up, please."

Kevin couldn't wait to get away from the Buzzard. He raced to get in line. As soon as his class had marched through the hall and exited the building, he felt freer. He took a deep breath. Their PE teacher, Mr. Pine, led them to the soccer field. "Today we're going to do some running. I want you to warm up by running around the field."

A few of the girls groaned, but Kevin was pleased. Running was something he could do. He didn't always have to pay attention, like in basketball or soccer. Or like he was supposed to do in the classroom.

"Come on. Get moving," said their teacher.

Kevin and some of the other boys set off like cheetahs chasing prey. "Run at an easy pace," their teacher said. "Move your arms and keep your shoulders relaxed."

Susan ran past him like a jackrabbit.

"This isn't a race," Mr. Pine shouted over the din of thudding feet. "There are no winners or losers. And if you feel tired or get a cramp, walk for a bit."

Kevin ran the first three lengths of the field at a steady pace. Ahead of him Susan slowed and began to walk. Kevin ran past her. He was feeling tired, too, but he wasn't going to slow down. He was breathing hard by the time they completed the run. Mr. Pine led them in some stretches. Kevin had no problem reaching toward his toes, but he noticed that Susan could touch the ground with both hands. Then they did head rolls, side stretches, torso twists, and jumping jacks.

"Okay, now," said their teacher, "I want to time all of you on the one-hundred-meter dash. I'll have you run two at a time, and I'll record your times. I won't grade you on this. I just want to see if you can improve your times if you run every day."

Kevin hoped he'd do better than most of the guys. It would be nice to be good at something.

"I'm going to have you run in alphabetical order. First up: Mike and Eliseo."

Mr. Pine led the first two runners to a spot on the field that he had marked with a big white line. "Place one foot just behind the line, then push off with your back foot. I've marked the spot that's exactly one hundred meters away from the starting line. I'm going to stand at the finish line with my stopwatch."

Their teacher jogged to the finish line, then blew his whistle. The two boys sped off. They ran almost neck and neck all the way. Mr. Pine was holding a clipboard and he wrote down their times. "Mike and Eliseo, you both ran the course in nineteen seconds. Next up: Susan and Jenny." He blew the whistle again.

Kevin was glad that Jenny finished ahead of Susan.

The teacher wrote down their times. "Jenny nineteen seconds, Susan twenty seconds. Next up: Richard and Kevin."

Kevin lined up beside Richard. He wondered what his time would be. Would he be faster? He heard the sharp tweet of the whistle and ran as fast as he could. Richard passed him running like a cheetah in pursuit of a gazelle. Kevin never caught up to him. When he crossed the finish line, Mr. Pine announced their times. "Richard twenty seconds and Kevin twenty-two."

Kevin frowned. He stood beside Mr. Pine and looked at the times for his classmates.

"Everyone is faster than me," said Kevin.

"It took several students twenty-three seconds. Don't worry. You can improve."

chapter nine

On Monday morning when Kevin entered the school, he saw Mr. Pine in the hall.

"I want to figure out how many miles per hour I can run if I run the one-hundred-meter dash in twenty-two seconds. Can you tell me how to do that?"

"Sure," said the PE teacher. "You can use a computer program. I'll get the name of that program and how to use it to you later today or tomorrow."

The final bell rang, so Kevin rushed to his classroom. He thrust his backpack under his desk, then hurried to the back of the room and tossed his coat into his cubby.

Susan and Rana were huddled with Mrs. Beezer

in the front of the room. The Buzzard was smiling, which meant she hadn't noticed him.

Kevin slumped into his seat.

"Did you find your snake yet?" Richard asked.

Kevin shook his head. "No, but I tried to lure him out. Last night I put a mouse inside a soda bottle."

"Sort of like a root beer float? But with a mouse instead of ice cream?" Richard raised his eyebrows and grinned.

Jenny had a horrified look on her face. "So the mouse was floating in the soda?"

"No, it was doing the backstroke," said Richard.

"Actually, the bottle was empty," said Kevin, unzipping his backpack, "and the mouse was dead." He pulled out the bottle and set it on his desk.

"Yuck." Jenny put her hand over her mouth and looked away.

Richard examined the bottle. "So you cut off the top section, put the mouse inside, then turned the top around and stuck it inside the bottle like a funnel."

"Right, so the snake could smell the mouse, but couldn't get it out," said Kevin. "Then I put the bottle on the floor in my room."

"What happened?" asked Richard.

"Nothing. I set my alarm and woke up every two hours, but the snake was never there." Kevin sighed.

Susan walked past Kevin's desk. She stopped and stared at the mouse bottle. "What in the world is that?"

"A cat toy," said Kevin. "Want one?"

Susan wrinkled her nose. "That's disgusting."

Kevin thrust the bottle into his backpack.

"Okay, class, everyone take your seats." Mrs. Beezer took roll, counted students for hot lunch, then started handing out graph paper. "This morning we're going to work on a graph to go with the page about your animal's diet."

"But Mrs. Steele said we only have to do one graph," Kevin said. He said it louder than he'd meant to.

The Buzzard glared at him. "You will be doing three graphs," she said firmly. "Most of you have already done one about your animal's size. The second one will have something to do with your animal's diet, and the third one will have something to do with an interesting fact about your animal."

"What about the pet graph we did yesterday?" said Kevin.

"That was just practice," said Mrs. Beezer.

Kevin moaned.

Richard leaned over and whispered. "You can work with us."

Kevin pushed his chair next to Richard's desk, then grabbed his graph paper.

"I found out that wild dogs can eat about ten pounds right after they've killed an animal," said Richard. "And Rana found out that lions can eat as much as sixty-five pounds."

"Wow, that's a lot," said Kevin.

"They have really big bellies after they eat that much," said Rana. "Do you know how much a cheetah can eat?"

Kevin shook his head.

"Well, take a guess," said Richard. "I'm sure Mrs. Beezer won't know how much they eat."

"But Mrs. Steele will probably know," said Kevin.

"You can always change it later," said Rana.

Kevin shrugged. "How about twenty pounds?"

"Sounds good to me." Richard started working on the graph.

Kevin went to the back of the room to sharpen his pencil.

When he got back to his chair, he saw Munchkin pull the plastic bottle out of his backpack and bat it with one paw. The bottle rolled sideways. The cat batted it again. The mouse flopped around in the bottle. The cat pounced on the bottle. Then he tried to get his paw into the bottle. He wanted to get the mouse. Somehow Munchkin hooked the top with a sharp claw and the top popped off. Students were standing in the aisle now, surrounding the cat.

"What's going on here?" said the Buzzard, pushing her way closer.

Munchkin pulled the mouse from the bottle, picked it up in his mouth, and raced out of the room.

The Buzzard picked up the bottle. "Does this belong to somebody in our class?" She looked around. "Kevin?"

Of course she'd blame him. Kevin shrugged his shoulders. "I don't know how it got here."

"Richard?" said the sub.

"Must have been that crazy cat," Richard said.

Jenny shot an angry glance at Kevin. Better to have her mad at him than the Buzzard.

Kevin logged on to the classroom computer and tried to find out how much a cheetah could eat at one time. But he got three different answers. Two places said cheetahs can eat six pounds of food, three said they can eat thirty pounds, and another one said twenty pounds.

When he got home, he wrote another e-mail.

> Dear Mrs. Steele,
>
> I did a Google search to find out how much a cheetah can eat, but I got three different answers: 6 pounds, 20 pounds, and 30 pounds. Which one is right?
>
> Your confused student,
> Kevin

chapter ten

On Tuesday morning the Buzzard called Kevin to her desk and handed him an envelope. "Mr. Pine said to give this to you." She had a puzzled look on her face.

Kevin tore the envelope open. "Cool. He sent me the Web address I wanted."

"Web address?" The Buzzard raised her eyebrows. They almost disappeared under her bangs.

"So I can figure out how fast I can run in miles per hour," Kevin explained. "I know I can run one hundred meters in twenty-two seconds."

Now her eyebrows were scrunched together. But all she said was, "Oh."

Kevin hurried to his desk before she could say anything else. He was glad that Mr. Pine hadn't forgotten about him.

After the morning announcements the Buzzard

said, "I have another e-mail from Mrs. Steele." She put on her glasses, picked up a sheet of paper, and began to read. "Today we took Byron, one of the trained cheetahs, to a school. We laughed when several people leaned out of their cars to say there was a cheetah in our van. Byron stood and looked out the van's side window during the hour-long ride to the school."

Kevin had read that cheetahs could see things three miles away. Did Byron see tasty animals in distant fields, or was he watching people in their cars?

The Buzzard read some more. "When we reached the school, we told the auditorium full of kids how cheetahs might possibly go extinct. Many farmers shoot them on sight because they blame cheetahs for killing their animals. But often the culprit is an animal that hunts at night, like a jackal."

The Buzzard looked at him. "Kevin," she said, "do you know when cheetahs hunt?"

"During the day," Kevin said. He wondered if she was surprised that he knew the right answer.

Mrs. Beezer nodded and continued reading. "Finally it was time for the kids to meet Byron. The cheetah strode gracefully into the room like visiting royalty. He'd visited many schools, so he wasn't scared at all."

Kevin wished a cheetah would walk into his classroom. The Buzzard would probably run away and not come back. He started drawing in his notebook.

He drew a cheetah striding into a room. Then he drew a woman with frizzy hair running away as she screamed, "Help! Help!"

"Mrs. Steele added a PS," said the Buzzard. "Here's an interesting fact I just learned about cheetahs. They can eat thirty pounds of meat after they make a kill. When they eat that much, their stomachs stick out like they've swallowed a basketball."

Thank you, Mrs. Steele, Kevin thought. Now he could fix his diet graph.

"Does anyone have any questions for Mrs. Steele?" the Buzzard asked.

Kevin raised his hand. The Buzzard glanced at him, then looked all around the room. No one else had a question. "Okay, Kevin," she finally said.

"When is Mrs. Steele coming back?"

"She flies home on Sunday. She'll be back in school next Monday. So I want everyone to finish their animal books by Friday. But right now we're going to do a math work sheet." She turned to her desk, picked up a stack of papers, and started handing them out.

Darn. Kevin still wasn't sure what to do for his last graph. He'd have to do some more research. But first he wanted to figure out his speed in miles per hour. He was dying to use the computer. Unfortunately, the Buzzard was explaining how to do the work sheet she'd just handed out. He twirled his pencil round and round. Jenny turned and glared at him. He stopped twirling the pencil. He looked at the clock and finished the work sheet quickly. Then he tilted his chair back until it hit the desk behind him.

Finally it was time to go to the library to work on their animal project. Eager to find out how he compared with other animals, Kevin asked the librarian for a book about animal speeds. Hurray! Nando found one for him. Kevin paged through it quickly. A rat could run six miles per hour and a mouse could run eight. He hoped that he ran faster than that.

Kevin sat down at a computer. He typed in the address of the speed conversion program. Then he typed in twenty-two seconds for his time running one hundred meters. The program showed that he had been running ten miles an hour. That was a lot less than a cheetah. He looked through the animal book. "I can run as fast as a crocodile," he told Richard.

Richard laughed. "Which animal runs as fast as I do?"

Kevin entered Richard's time of twenty seconds. The program computed his speed at eleven miles per hour. "That's how fast a pig runs."

Richard laughed again. "I don't want to be a pig." Then he made oinking sounds.

Eliseo was using the computer next to them. "What are you guys doing?" he asked.

"We're figuring out how fast we run compared with various animals," explained Richard. "How many seconds did it take you to run one hundred meters?"

"I think it was nineteen seconds," said Eliseo.

Kevin entered Eliseo's time. The program computed his speed at twelve miles per hour. "That's how fast a squirrel and a black mamba snake can run."

Eliseo rolled his eyes. "How can a snake move that fast? It doesn't have legs."

Kevin went to Google and typed in the question. "It says snakes use their scales to move. Here are some YouTube videos of black mambas moving."

"Let's watch one," said Richard.

"Look at that," Kevin pointed to the screen. "Black mambas can move with a third of their body raised off the ground."

Richard shivered. "I'm going to have nightmares about that thing chasing me."

The Buzzard was suddenly behind them. "Too much chitter-chatter," she spat like a cobra spraying venom.

Kevin glared at her back as she hissed at someone else. The Buzzard gave *him* nightmares.

At PE class that afternoon Kevin thanked Mr. Pine for the conversion information. "I figured out that I can run ten miles an hour, as fast as a crocodile."

Mr. Pine laughed. "You have a very creative mind."

Kevin was surprised. "The Buzzard—I mean, Mrs. Beezer thinks I get too distracted all the time."

"I have that problem, too."

"You do?"

Mr. Pine nodded. "Running helps me focus. It

would probably help you, too." He blew his whistle. "Okay, class, let's run some laps."

Kevin ran with purpose now. He wanted to get faster, and he wanted to do a good job on his animal book. For Mrs. Steele. He knew he couldn't please the Buzzard.

When class was over, Kevin walked into the building with Mr. Pine.

"I want to run faster," Kevin told him.

"I think you can do that. Run at recess every day. Good runners spend a lot of time training."

"How fast can a good runner do one hundred meters?" asked Kevin.

"A star football player can run it in about twelve seconds. The fastest Olympic runners can run it in about nine and a half seconds."

"I'd like to run it in nineteen seconds," Kevin said. "That's how fast a black mamba can move."

Mr. Pine smiled. "Run every day. See if that helps you with your schoolwork, too."

As soon as he entered the classroom, Kevin headed for the class computer. He entered the time for the fastest Olympic runners and found out that they could run twenty-three miles per hour. Wow! It wasn't even close to a cheetah's speed, but it was a whole lot faster than he could run.

"Kevin, are you doing schoolwork or something else?"

The Buzzard was leaning over his shoulder.

Kevin knew she could see that he wasn't working on cheetahs. "I ca-can run as fast as a crocodile," he stammered.

"But what does that have to do with cheetahs?" the Buzzard said in a stern voice. "And where is your second math graph?"

Kevin pulled a wrinkled piece of paper from his desk. "I'd really like to do something better than this," he said. "Something really different."

"Well, you'd better figure something out very soon." She looked at the graph on his desk and frowned. "And you'll have to redo this graph. It's too messy."

Kevin put his head down on the desk. Nothing he did was ever good enough for the Buzzard.

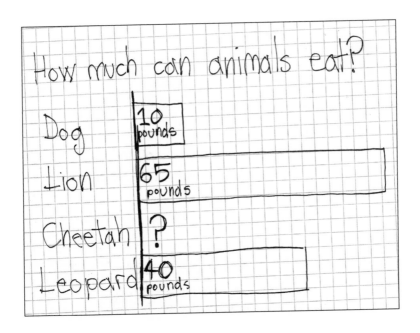

chapter eleven

On Wednesday morning Kevin joined the throng of kids who rushed onto the playground for recess. Several boys gathered by the basketball hoop and practiced tossing the ball into the net. A group of girls sat on the swings and talked.

Kevin walked slowly to the edge of the soccer field and took a deep breath. He'd promised Mr. Pine he'd run every day, but he worried that he'd look silly running by himself. He walked fast at first, then broke into a run. He kept his eyes down and placed each foot carefully. He'd really look like a dork if he tripped and fell.

As he completed his first lap around the field he noticed several kids staring at him. Just run, he told himself. Did the world's fastest man worry about people staring? No. The kids staring at him were probably wondering how he could possibly run so slowly.

Suddenly Richard was beside him. "Passing the crocodile," he said as he raced ahead.

Kevin laughed and ran faster. He remembered that Richard could run as fast as a pig. "Oink," he said as he passed Richard.

Richard caught up, and they raced side by side. Halfway through the lap they were both puffing. "Time to slow down," said Kevin.

Richard nodded in agreement, and they both walked for a while.

"Let's try a rat's pace," said Kevin. "That's six miles an hour."

Richard grinned. "Good plan," he said, and they ran the next several laps at a slow, easy pace.

After recess they all worked on a math work sheet. Kevin finished his quickly, then began to work on a graph about animal speeds. He used the back of one of his messy graphs to sketch out his new idea. He started with a bar for a crocodile at ten miles per hour, then a pig at eleven, a black mamba at twelve, and an elephant at fifteen miles per hour. He put in a bar for the fastest human runners. After that he added bars for lions, leopards, wild dogs, hyenas, zebras, gazelles, and finally, the fastest land animals, the cheetahs. He wrote the title in capital letters: "HOW FAST CAN YOUR ANIMAL RUN?"

He showed the bar graph to Richard.

"I'd like a speed graph like that for my book," said Richard. "Would you mind?"

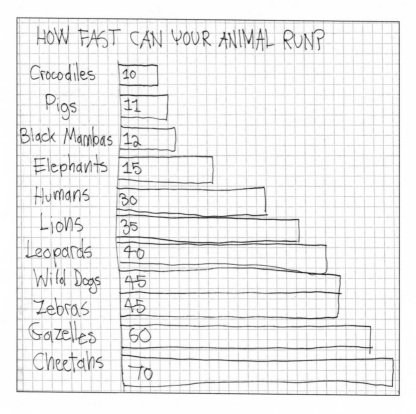

HOW FAST CAN YOUR ANIMAL RUN?

Animal	Speed
Crocodiles	10
Pigs	11
Black Mambas	12
Elephants	15
Humans	30
Lions	35
Leopards	40
Wild Dogs	45
Zebras	45
Gazelles	60
Cheetahs	70

"No, I'm glad you like it," said Kevin. "Can you help me put it on the computer so it's not messy?"

During computer lab they used the graphing program to draw the graph and printed out two copies. When Rana walked by and saw the graph, she wanted one, too. So did Eliseo.

"Just don't tell Mrs. Beezer that it was my idea," said Kevin, "because then she wouldn't like it."

"But it's a good idea," said Rana.

Eliseo said, "I really like it, too."

chapter twelve

On Friday morning Kevin didn't get a chance to give Munchkin his usual tuna treat. He'd checked the library, but the cat wasn't there. He didn't see the cat until they went out for morning recess. Munchkin was across the street peering intently into some bushes. When Kevin called him, the cat came running and quickly ate his tuna treat.

"You should put Munchkin on the speed graph," Jenny said. She tried to get the cat to run around the soccer field with them, but instead, Munchkin sprinted back to the same bushes where he'd been earlier.

"That's a good idea," said Richard, "even though Munchkin won't run with us."

"The cat doesn't need to build up his speed," said Kevin. "He already runs thirty miles per hour."

"Is that really how fast a house cat can run?" asked Jenny.

Kevin nodded. "That's why they're so good at catching mice."

Jenny kept pace with Kevin and Richard as they finished their first lap. More and more students began to join them. By the time they ran their second lap around the field, around a dozen kids ran with them. Most were students from their class, but there were a few younger kids as well.

After lunch the Buzzard had them gather on the rug.

"Let's share interesting facts about your animals," Mrs. Beezer said. "Susan, why don't you begin?"

"A silverback gorilla takes care of the others in his troop. There can be as many as thirty animals in a troop."

"Is that like a Girl Scout troop?" asked Richard.

Susan gave him a dirty look. "A group of gorillas is called a troop. And do you know why they call the big male a silverback? It's because he has a band of silver hair on his back."

"Very good, Susan," said the teacher. "Who wants to go next? Jenny?"

"Leopards hunt at night. When a leopard kills an animal, it often drags it high into a tree so lions and hyenas can't steal it."

"Nice, Jenny," said the Buzzard. "Can you imagine how strong a leopard has to be to do that?"

"Leopards have strong jaws and big shoulder muscles," Jenny said.

"Hyenas have very strong jaws," said Eliseo. "They eat every part of an animal, even skin and bones. Their poops are white because they eat so many bones."

Some of the kids giggled.

"I'm glad to know that, Eliseo," said the Buzzard with a smile.

Rana raised her hand. "A lion can run much faster than I can. They can run thirty-five miles an hour. I can only run eleven miles per hour."

"Good thing we don't have any lions wandering around outside, isn't it?" said the Buzzard. "I like how you compared your own speed with a lion's speed. Did you put the information on a graph?"

Rana nodded.

"How did you figure out your speed?" the teacher asked.

"Mr. Pine timed us when we ran the one-hundred-meter dash. There's a program on the computer where you can plug in your time. Then it figures out your speed in miles per hour."

"Good work, Rana."

Kevin wondered if the Buzzard would still like the idea if she knew he was the one who thought of it.

Suddenly, the Buzzard gasped, stood up, and moved quickly toward the back of the room.

Kevin looked around. Munchkin stood next to him. The cat held a wriggling snake in his mouth.

"Did you bring me a present?" asked Kevin.

Munchkin dropped the snake on the floor. The cat pushed the snake with his paw.

Several girls screamed and scurried away. One girl sat on a desktop, clutching her feet close to her body.

Kevin reached over and grabbed the snake's head with one hand and the body with the other. "It's just a garter snake," he said.

"Keep it away from me." Jenny got to her feet and backed away.

Kevin studied the snake. "I think it's hurt. The poor thing has two puncture wounds from being picked up by the cat, so we can't just let it go."

"Oh dear," said the Buzzard.

Munchkin climbed onto Kevin's lap and reached for the snake.

Kevin held the snake away. "Will somebody please take the cat?" he asked.

"Come here, you rascal." Richard picked the cat up.

Munchkin struggled to get down.

"Here, take him before he claws me," said Richard, handing the squirming cat to Jenny.

"The snake needs to go to Reptile Rescue," said Kevin. "My mother is taking me there after school anyway."

"Are you going to get another snake?" asked Richard.

"No, we're going to take my pet snake there."

"You found him?" asked Jenny.

"I put a heating pad on the couch last night," Kevin explained. "The snake was lying on it this morning."

"Aren't you sad about losing your snake?" asked Jenny.

"No, I've talked to my mother about getting a kitten for a pet." Kevin smiled. "My mom thought that was a good idea."

"Munchkin won you over, didn't he?" said Jenny.

"He sure did," said Kevin.

"What are you going to do with the snake?" The Buzzard was still standing by the window. "You can't just hold him for the rest of the day."

"I can put him in my backpack," said Kevin, "but first I need to dump everything else out."

"I'll do that for you," said Richard.

"The snake won't escape, will it?" asked the Buzzard.

"If it does, I'll just catch it again," said Kevin.

After Kevin had put the snake in his backpack and zipped it securely, the Buzzard said, "Thank you so much." She gave him a strained smile. "I don't like snakes."

chapter thirteen

On Monday Kevin was early to school for once. He couldn't wait to see Mrs. Steele. But what if her plane had been delayed, or even canceled? She might still be in Africa. He was afraid he'd throw up his breakfast if he walked into school and saw the Buzzard. Just thinking about it made his stomach queasy.

He waited outside on the playground for the first bell to ring. Jenny and Richard stood with him.

"Did you get a new pet yet?" Jenny asked.

Kevin nodded. "After we dropped off both snakes, we went to see about cat adoptions. I picked a gray kitten because she purred when I held her."

"That's a very good sign," said Jenny.

"We bought a bed for her, but she wouldn't stay

in it," Kevin told them. "I left my door open, and she jumped on my bed and slept with me."

"See, I told you a cat was a better pet than a snake," said Jenny. "You never slept with your snake, did you?"

"I like snakes, but not enough to sleep with one."

Jenny shivered. "Just the thought of it gives me the creeps."

Finally, the bell rang and they entered the school together. Kevin held his breath as he entered the classroom. And there was Mrs. Steele. She looked more beautiful than ever, and when she smiled at him, it was a real smile. Even her eyes were smiling. Kevin was so glad to see her that he thought about hugging her. Instead, he just said, "Hi," and walked quickly back to his cubby.

"Did you bring us a real live cheetah?" Richard asked.

Mrs. Steele laughed. "I did bring some cheetah pictures to show you. But first, I want to see your animal books."

Kevin was afraid she wouldn't like his messy handwriting. Or maybe she wouldn't be excited about his graph.

Mrs. Steele had something nice to say about everybody's book.

"Eliseo, I like all your graphs," she told him, "but the animal speed graph is especially nice, since it includes many of the African animals we're studying.

And you've compared a hyena's speed with your own speed, which is a nice touch."

Oh no! Now Eliseo was getting credit for Kevin's speed graph.

But Eliseo was very kind. "It was Kevin's idea," he told their teacher.

"Really?" said Mrs. Steele. She turned and looked at him.

Didn't his favorite teacher believe he could do something good?

"Show me your graphs, Kevin," said his teacher, leaning over his desk. She smiled warmly, so maybe she did believe Eliseo.

He laid his three graphs on his desk.

"Good work, Kevin," Mrs. Steele said. "I can see that you contributed to the diet graph." She winked at him. "And I love your speed graph! It's such a creative idea! I'm so pleased that you shared your idea with other students."

Kevin sighed with relief. It was great to have his teacher back. For the past two weeks he'd felt like a total dunce.

Mrs. Steele stood up straight and looked around the room. "Hmm. If we moved Susan and Mary's graph to the smaller bulletin board, then you could make a big speed graph for the back bulletin board."

Kevin gulped. "I've never done a big graph like that." He'd be happy to replace Susan's graph, but he was afraid he'd make a big, sloppy mess.

Mrs. Steele understood immediately. "Rana and Jenny will help, won't you girls? And Richard and Eliseo, you'll both help, won't you?" said Mrs. Steele. "Kevin," she went on, "I love your drawing of a cheetah running. Could you make a big cheetah drawing to place above the graph?"

"Sure, I'd like to do that," Kevin said. No wonder he'd missed Mrs. Steele so much. She did believe in him. He felt like he did at Christmas when he got just the right gift.

Later that day Mrs. Steele joined them outside for their PE class with Mr. Pine.

"Are you going to run with us?" Kevin asked.

"No, I'm not going to run today," Mrs. Steele said, "but maybe I'll join you when I get over my jet lag."

Mrs. Steele stood with Mr. Pine while the class ran their warm-up laps. When they lined up for the one-hundred-meter run, she stood at the finish line and yelled encouragement to each of the runners.

Finally, Kevin and Richard were up. Kevin hoped he could beat his "crocodile" time. With Mrs. Steele cheering him on, he was bound to do better. But Richard still finished first.

"Nineteen seconds, Richard," said Mr. Pine. "Good job. You cut your time by one second."

"You ran as fast as a black mamba," Kevin told his friend.

"Should I hiss?" asked Richard, grinning.

"Twenty seconds. Way to go, Kevin," said Mr. Pine. "You cut your time by two seconds."

"Congratulations," said Richard. "You ran as fast as a pig!"

"Oink," said Kevin happily.